BOOM Chicka R

To sweet Cinder and the boys:
    Arie, Kevin, Michael, and Valde. You rock!   —JA

To my Boom Chicka, Dawson Lee Chitwood   —STC

PATRICIA LEE GAUCH, EDITOR

No part of this publication may be reproduced in whole or in part, or stored in a retrieval system,
or transmitted in any form or by any means, electronic, mechanical, photocopying, recording,
or otherwise, without written permission of the publisher. For information regarding permission,
write to Philomel Books, an imprint of Penguin Putnam Books for Young Readers,
a division of Penguin Group (USA) Inc., 345 Hudson Street, New York, NY 10014.
ISBN 0-439-69136-2
Text copyright © 2004 by John Archambault. Illustrations copyright © 2004 by Suzanne Tanner Chitwood.
All rights reserved. Published by Scholastic Inc., 557 Broadway, New York, NY 10012, by arrangement with
Philomel Books, an imprint of Penguin Putnam Books for Young Readers, a division of Penguin Group (USA) Inc.
SCHOLASTIC and associated logos are trademarks and/or registered trademarks of Scholastic Inc.
12 11 10 9 8 7 6 5 4 3 2 1   5 6 7 8 9/0
Printed in Mexico   e   46
First Scholastic printing, September 2004.
Designed by Semadar Megged
Text set in 26-point Skippy Sharp
The art was done in torn paper collage.

OCK

John Archambault

illustrated by SUZANNE TANNER CHITWOOD

The mouse stepped out of his little mouse hole
   To see what was left in the cereal bowl.
He looked this way and pip-squeaked that
He said, "No sign of Max the cat.

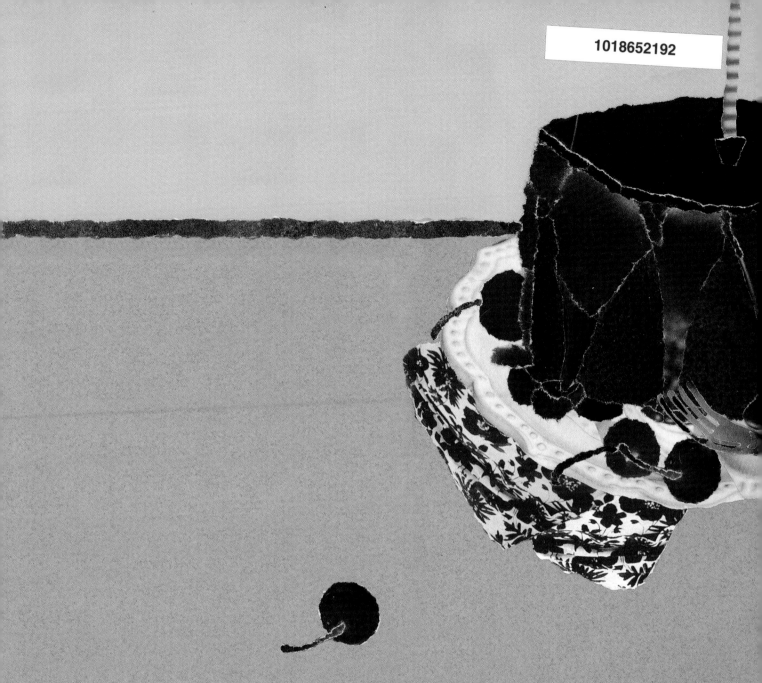

"I spy Birthday Cake on the old buffet.
The cat's asleep. It's time to play!
Let's dance and party and Rock-and-Roll.
Bring out the Good China Dishes
    and the Big Punch Bowl!"

Tip-toe, tip-toe, rickety-rock.

"Let's sneak away from the kitchen clock!"

"Lion's asleep," said Hour Number ONE.
"Now's our chance to have some fun!"
"I'm with you," said Number TWO.
"My left foot's dancing in my right-foot shoe!"

Everybody rock! Around the room!

Boom Chicka Rock, Chicka Rock, Chicka Boom!

"No, not me," said Number
THREE.
"I don't want Lion coming
after me!"

"Let him roar," said Number FOUR.
"We're gonna Boogie-Woogie 'cross the dining-room floor."

"Sakes alive!" cried Number FIVE.
"He'll be churning up a storm in the old beehive."
"Fiddlesticks," said Number SIX.
"We'll throw him by the tail into the pancake mix."

Everybody rock! Around the room!

"My engine's revvin'," said Number SEVEN.
"But the cat's in the way of the old buffet!
He fell asleep on the Queen Anne chair,
Dreaming of mice he hopes to scare!"

"No time to wait!" said Number EIGHT.
"Climb over the Lion before it's too late
And Jitterbug over to the Birthday Cake!"

"Hands on your hips," said Number NINE.
"We're gonna Bunny Hop, do the Conga Line.
That Birthday Cake is mine, all mine!"

"Fast as you can!" said Number TEN.
"Let's Electric Slide through the Lion's den!
I'm Big Daddy, Dancing Daddy, double-digit Ten—
Lion can't catch me and I'll say it again.
Come with me, Cousin ELEVEN.
We'll waltz by Max into Midnight Heaven."

Everybody rock! Around the room!

Boom Chicka Rock,

Chicka Rock,

Chicka Boom!

Big hand, little hand, straight up—
TWELVE O'clock.
It's midnight, tip-toe, rickety-rock.
Counting our way 'round the kitchen clock.

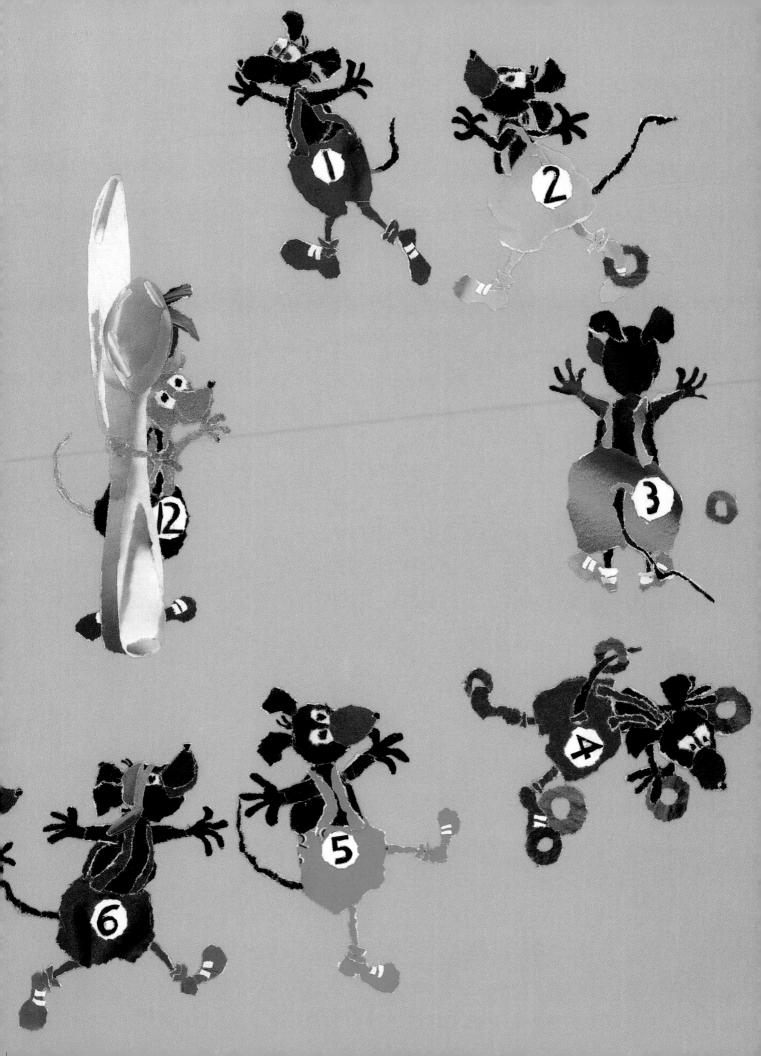

ONE, TWO,

THREE O'clock,

FOUR

Sweeping up crumbs on the kitchen floor.

FIVE, SIX,

SEVEN O'clock,

EIGHT

Mice feet dancing on the Good China Plate.

NINE, TEN,

ELEVEN O'clock,

TWELVE

Now the mouse is swinging on the dinner bell!

The clock struck twelve. "Oh, no! Oh, dear!"
The midnight mouse is pulling Max's ear!
The midnight mouse—Number TWELVE—
Brave and brash, started to yell,
"Let's jump rope with the Lion's tail!"

Kitty cat Lion Max. Listen to him purr.
Cut the cake! Put icing on his whiskers and fur!

Griff, Gruff, Growl . . .

"Lion's awake!" said Number ONE.
"Everybody listen to me—everybody run!
He's looking for us in the goldfish bowl.
We just slipped through the doughnut hole."

Let's all Tango, do the Fandango,
Tip-toe, tip-toe, rickety-rock
Sock Hop back to the kitchen clock.
Zing! Zang!
Boomerang!

Tomorrow can't begin
Till every hour is home
And every number's tucked in.

ONE, TWO,
THREE O'clock,
FOUR
"Hurry up! Open up the cuckoo-clock door!"
FIVE, SIX,
SEVEN O'clock,
EIGHT
"Midnight, bedtime. Way too late!"
NINE, TEN,
ELEVEN O'clock,
TWELVE

"Scurry, hurry, quick, hear Max's bell!"
Ding-A-Ling Dong! Sing a good-night song—
   with a whisper.

Everybody rock! Around the room!

Boom Chicka Rock, Chicka Rock, Chicka Boom!

Every hour is home. Every number's
   tucked in.
The last stroke of twelve, now
   tomorrow can begin!

Ding-A-Ling Dong!

Hear Max's bell.

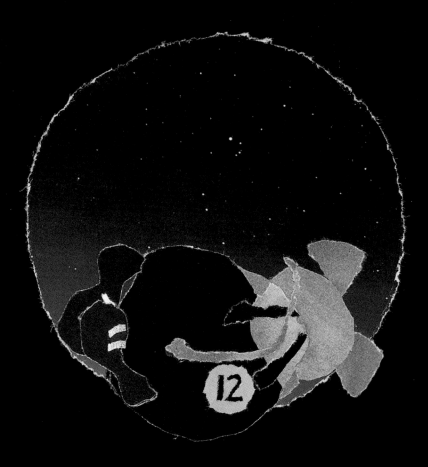

He's pawing at the clock—midnight!

And all is well.